D1245278

NICE SHOES!

Charleston, SC
www.PalmettoPublishing.com

Nice Shoes!
Copyright © © 2022 by Dennis Gillan & Stephen Pihl

All rights reserved

No portion of this book may be reproduced, stored
in a retrieval system, or transmitted in any form by any
means—electronic, mechanical, photocopy, recording, or
other—except for brief quotations in printed reviews, without
prior permission of the author.

First Edition

Hardcover ISBN: 978-1-68515-695-4
Paperback ISBN: 978-1-68515-696-1
eBook ISBN: 978-1-68515-697-8

NiCE SHOES!

A little compliment can go a long way

Based on a True Story

Dennis Gillan, Stephen Pihl

Derek had three older brothers, so he rarely got new clothes. He got hand-me-downs, and that was OK. He enjoyed dressing like his brothers. Today was different because his mom came home with brand new sneakers just for him!

Derek was so excited about wearing his new shoes that he could barely sleep. He woke up late for school, so he had no time to eat his favorite breakfast—waffles!

His brothers ate hot waffles, while he had to eat cold cereal so he could

catch the bus—and his brothers did
not notice his new shoes.

Derek's new shoes made him run so fast that he caught the bus *just* in time. "Hopefully today will get better," he thought to himself. As he was getting off the bus at school, he tripped on the last step and fell onto the ground. Everyone was laughing at him as he got up and hurried inside.

Nobody helped Derek, and no one noticed his new shoes.

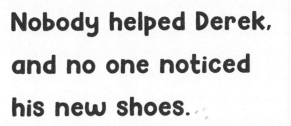

WELCOME BACK! Go Eagles

Oh no! Derek forgot that he had gym class today.

6

He had his new shoes but no gym uniform, so he wasn't allowed to play. His friends picked on him about forgetting his gym clothes and talked about how much fun they had playing his favorite game—basketball. Derek was even sadder. Real friends wouldn't pick on him, and still no one noticed his new shoes!

In math class, Derek had a pop quiz. He did not do so well.

8

He passed the quiz, but he knew he could do better. He kept thinking about the answers he got wrong and how still no one noticed his new shoes.

Derek then went to science class, and when his science teacher went around to collect the homework, Derek realized that he had forgotten it at home! Derek loved science, and he had worked hard on the homework assignment. Derek's day was getting worse, and *still* nobody noticed his new shoes!

Lunchtime! As Derek was eating his lunch, he spilled chocolate milk all over his shirt. He ran to the bathroom to clean it off. Derek was looking in the mirror, thinking about how badly this day was going so far. He felt like things would only get worse and he may never be happy again. It was like the world wanted him to be sad forever. And on top of it all, no one noticed his new shoes.

Derek loved band class, and he was a good musician. Unfortunately, today his music teacher was sick, and the class did not get to play their instruments. They watched a movie about music instead of making music. This made Derek even sadder, and with the lights turned down for the movie, no one noticed his new shoes.

At the end of the day, Derek was walking out of school and was having bad thoughts. He was telling himself that he was not a good person or a good student. Derek wanted this day to end. He started to worry that every day would be like this. He even stopped caring about his new shoes.

On the way to the bus, the most popular kid in school, Carlos, was walking right towards Derek. Derek tried to get out of his way, but he and Carlos kept moving in the same direction. Derek was really embarrassed and just wanted this day to be over. Then Carlos chuckled, and as Derek waited for what he thought was going to be a mean comment, Carlos said, "Hey, Derek. Nice shoes. Are those new? They are really cool."

Derek was shocked that he was getting a compliment! Then Carlos said "Really, dude, nice shoes!"

Carlos put out his hand and they fist bumped. Derek finally smiled and realized that his day wasn't so bad after all.

Carlos was the most popular kid in school because he was also the nicest kid in school. Even though Derek had a rough day, he left school with happy thoughts, all because of one compliment: *NICE SHOES*.

Be kind to others because you never know what they are going through, and you just might make their day!

Based on a true story.

Made in the USA
Columbia, SC
13 August 2022

65153963R00015